Raggedy Ann and Andy

and the
RAINY-DAY CIRCUS

by Barbara Shook Hazen

illustrated by June Goldsborough

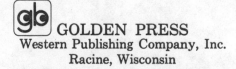

GOLDEN PRESS
Western Publishing Company, Inc.
Racine, Wisconsin

Copyright © 1973 by The Bobbs-Merrill Company, Inc.
Printed in U.S.A. by Western Publishing Company, Inc.
All rights reserved.

Fifth Printing, 1977

Marcella propped Raggedy Ann and Andy, hand-in-hand, on the nursery window seat.

"Please don't be sad," she said. "I wish I could take you to the circus with me, but it's too wet outside. You'd get all soggy."

Marcella put the rest of the dolls in their places on the shelf. Then she tucked Fido in his dog bed and Boots in her kitty basket.

"Good-bye, my dears." Marcella waved from the door. "I'll be home soon."

Raggedy Ann winked at Andy. "Just wait," she whispered. "We're going to have a circus here, too."

The very second the door closed, the nursery sprang to life.

"Forward, march!" Soldier Doll shouted as he led his troops out of their shoe box barracks.

Clown Doll danced for joy, Cowboy Doll galloped after a bandit, and Fireman Doll raced his truck out of the little red firehouse. "Clang! Clang! Here I come!" he called.

"Quiet, everyone," said Raggedy Ann. "I have a surprise. We can have our own rainy-day circus—right here in the nursery!"

"We can use the sheets from Marcella's bed for a circus tent," added Andy.

"And we can build benches out of the blocks," said Soldier Doll.

"Hurray!" cheered the dolls.

Everyone helped. Raggedy Ann and Andy put up the tent, and Soldier Doll and his troops built sturdy block benches.

French Doll and Ballerina Doll made the cotton candy—and Fido licked the pan.

Soon everyone was sitting under the "big top."
Rum-te-tum, rum-te-tum! blared the military march-
ing band. "Our rainy-day circus has just begun!"

First came a colorful parade of clowns and stuffed wild animals. There were lions and tigers and pelicans and teddy bears—and a pink elephant on roller skates. "Isn't he funny?" giggled Raggedy Ann.

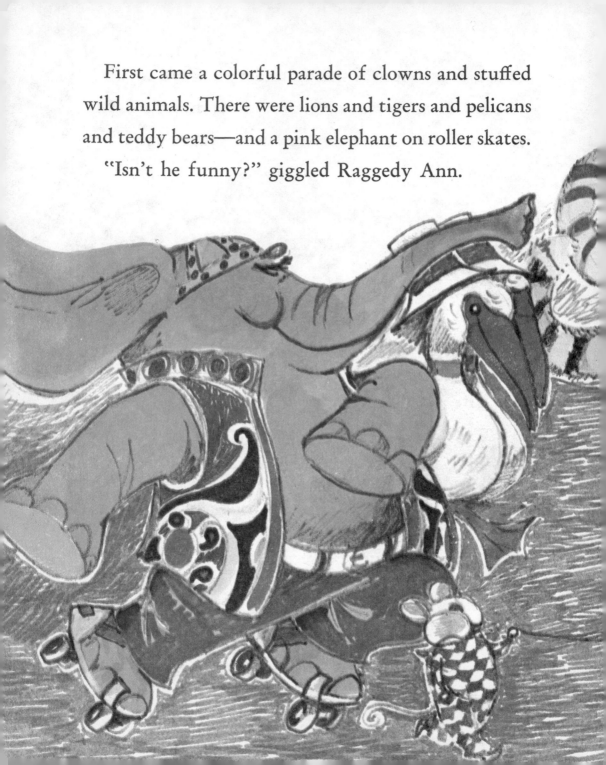

Cowboy Doll was first on the program. He per-
formed daring lasso tricks on Poncho, his painted
hobbyhorse.

"Yippee-ai-ay!" Cowboy Doll called as he twirled
his lariat.

French Doll was next. Everyone oohed and aahed as she tiptoed across the tightrope.

"Woof! Woof!" barked Fido. "Watch my juggling-dog act." Then, to show how good he was, Fido juggled six dog biscuits at once, while balancing a ball on the tip of his nose.

"Meow, meow," mewed Boots. "I'm the marvel-ous cat on the flying trapeze. Watch me float through the air with the greatest of ease."

After Boots did her act, the crowd began to chant, "We want Raggedy Ann and Andy. We want Raggedy Ann and Andy!"

But the Raggedys were nowhere to be seen. Instead, the next act turned out to be a horse—a horse with red and white striped stockings!

The band began to play as the horse skipped and hopped and circled the ring. When the horse marched to the center of the ring, the band stopped playing.

"For my first trick," said the horse, "I will count to five."

"A talking horse!" cried Clown Doll.

The horse tapped one front foot five times as he counted. "One, two, three, four, five." Then he bowed a long, low bow.

"A horse that can count!" cried French Doll. Everyone clapped and clapped.

"For my next trick," said the horse, "I will change my size." The horse's front feet walked forward, his back feet walked backward, and he became longer . . . and longer . . . and longer! Everyone shouted and cheered.

The drums began to roll. Then the horse made his front feet hop backward and his back feet hop forward, and suddenly he was short and fat! Again he bowed a long, low bow.

The cheering was so loud that, at first, no one heard Fido bark. "Woof! Woof!" warned Fido. "Marcella's coming home!"

"Move fast!" cried Soldier Doll. "We must put everything back the way it was."

"But where are Raggedy Ann and Andy?" asked Cowboy Doll.

"Here we are!" said two voices.

Then the front half of the horse with the red and white striped stockings hurried off. It was Raggedy Ann! "I'll take down the circus tent!" she cried.

Raggedy Andy climbed out of his half of the horse costume. "I'll help Cowboy Doll round up the hobbyhorses," he said.

The nursery door opened just a second after the dolls had scurried to their places.

"Funny," said Marcella, looking around. "I thought I heard something, but everything is just the way I left it."

Then she said, "Poor rag dolls. I'm sorry you had such a dull rainy day."

But the dolls all smiled contentedly. They were remembering the lasso tricks and the tightrope walker and the juggling dog and the cat on the flying trapeze —and the longest, shortest, fattest, funniest, most wonderful horse in the world—a horse with red and white striped stockings.